First published in 2001 in Great Britain by Gullane Children's Books
This paperback edition published in 2006 by

Gullane Children's Books
an imprint of Pinwheel Limited, Winchester House,
259-269 Old Marylebone Road,
London NW1 5XJ

1 3 5 7 9 10 8 6 4 2

Text © Sally Grindley 2001
Illustrations © Thomas Taylor 2001

The right of Sally Grindley and Thomas Taylor to be identified
as the author and illustrator of this work has been asserted by them
in accordance with the Copyright, Designs and Patents Act, 1988.

A CIP record for this title is available from the British Library.

ISBN-13: 978-1-86233-425-0
ISBN-10: 1-86233-425-0

Printed and bound in Singapore

The Sorcerer's Apprentice

Retold by **Sally Grindley**

Illustrated by **Thomas Taylor**

GULLANE
CHILDREN'S BOOKS

In an old stone castle, surrounded by whispering trees and gawping crows, lived a powerful sorcerer. He had been there for as long as anyone could remember, but few people had met him, and no-one had ever been invited through the castle's solid oak door. No-one except the sorcerer's apprentice.

The apprentice had been chosen by the sorcerer to help him.

"Work hard, my friend," the sorcerer had said to him, "and in time I will teach you everything I know."

The apprentice couldn't wait to follow in his master's magic steps, and was happy to do everything he was asked.

He spent hours in the woods digging up worms and catching rare beetles. He collected tree bark and plant roots until his hands were sore and his back aching.

Back in the castle kitchen, he crushed and ground them into powder.

And when he had finished, he rushed up and down stairs tidying and cleaning up after his master.

Sometimes, late at night while his master slept, the apprentice would creep into the sorcerer's laboratory. He was fascinated by the sight of the benches loaded with flagons and flasks and jars and phials in all shapes and sizes. The shelves were piled high with powders and potions, minerals and herbs, gems and ores. There were scales for measuring, bowls for mixing, strainers for sifting and pans for boiling.

The apprentice would wave his arms about and mutter magical-sounding words, pretending to make spells, while mixing drops of liquid the sorcerer had left for him to tidy away. He longed for the time when he could make real magic.

"One day, I'm going to be a great magician," he told the sorcerer's cat. "Just you wait and see."

But every time the apprentice asked to be allowed to try a spell, the sorcerer would reply, "Patience, my friend. It has taken me a whole lifetime to learn the secrets of my science. Your time will come."

The apprentice tried to be patient, but as the months passed by he grew more and more discontented.

"I'll be an old man before he lets me do any spells," he grumbled to the sorcerer's cat.

Then, one morning, the sorcerer
called the apprentice to him.
"I am going across the hills to
visit a great sorcerer friend,"
he said. "I shall need plenty of
hot water when I return at dusk.
Please fill our largest cauldron
ready for me."

The apprentice sat
down miserably.
"It will take me a
hundred trips to the well
to fill up the cauldron."
Then he had an idea.

As soon as the sorcerer had left, the apprentice crept into the great hall and pulled out one of the ancient spell books he had seen his master reading. He pulled out another, and flicked through them all until, at last, he stopped and shrieked with excitement. "This is it!" he cried. "I'll show my master that I'm ready!"

The apprentice raced back to the kitchen
and picked up an old broomstick.

"Watch this!" he called to the sorcerer's cat.
He grasped the broomstick tightly with
both hands, took a deep breath and said . . .

"Broomstick, listen to my spell,
Fetch me water from the well,
Fill the cauldron to the top,
Keep on going till I tell you Stop!"

Then he closed his eyes
and carefully chanted
seven magic words . . .

The broomstick leapt from his hands. The apprentice watched in amazement as it grew arms and legs.

He stared with wonder as it flung open the castle's huge oak doors and marched off down the path to the well.

He gasped with astonishment as it filled two buckets
with water, marched back up the path, through the
doors, down the steps and into the castle kitchen.
It emptied the buckets into the cauldron
and set off again for the well.

The apprentice clapped
his hands with glee.
"I've done it!" he cried
to the sorcerer's cat.
"I can make magic."
The sorcerer's cat
fled from the castle.

The apprentice sat down to watch the broomstick at work. Back it came with more water, then off again to the well. Back and forth. Back and forth.

He began to think of all the other spells he would try. Soon he was carried away wit dreams of turning pebbles int sticky toffees, making the sun shine in the night, paddling in rivers of gold . . .

The apprentice woke
with a start. Paddling? He
looked down. The kitchen
floor was covered with water.
The broomstick was just
emptying two more buckets
into the cauldron, which
was already overflowing.

"Stop! Stop!"
shrieked the apprentice.
The broomstick marched
on across the floor.
"Stop when I tell you!"
cried the apprentice again.
But the broomstick just
climbed the steps and went
out through the huge doors.

The apprentice found to his horror that he
couldn't remember the magic words that would
break the spell. He ran down the path shouting
after the broomstick. But nothing would stop it.
In desperation, the apprentice grabbed
the axe that he used for cutting firewood.
As the broomstick emptied the bucket,
he chopped it into dozens of pieces.

But . . . no sooner had the pieces fallen, than they too grew arms and legs, leapt to their feet and marched off to the well. Then back they came, a whole army of them. They shoved past the apprentice and marched relentlessly onwards, determined to carry out his command.

The waters rose up and up. The apprentice cried out with terror. He lost his footing and fell – splash! – into the water.

"Help!" he cried. "Help me!"

And help came.

A powerful voice bellowed
seven magic words.

Everything fell still.

Then, in a flash, the water simply swirled away.
The broomstick gathered up all its pieces and
sloped off to the corner of the kitchen. The pieces
joined together and the arms and legs disappeared.

The apprentice stood in the middle
of the room, dripping wet and shivering.
  "I trusted you," said the sorcerer quietly.
  "I'm sorry, sir," whispered the apprentice.
"I have let you down."

"You have been very foolish to meddle with things you don't understand," said the sorcerer. "Only the wise may share the secrets of the universe. I should send you away."

"Just one chance is all I ask," pleaded the apprentice. "I know I will be a good magician, I know it."

The sorcerer looked at his apprentice and saw the eagerness in his eyes.

"Perhaps I have held you back for too long," he said. "I will give you one chance, but be sure you reach out and grab it with both hands."

"I will, I promise!" cried the apprentice.
"Then come with me," replied the sorcerer,
"and we will make a start."